Strange and
Spooky Stories

Published in the United States in 1997 by The Millbrook Press, Inc.
2 Old New Milford Road, Brookfield, CT 06804

First published in Great Britain in 1997 by Barefoot Books, Ltd.
PO Box 95, Kingswood, Bristol BS15 5BH, Great Britain

Designed by Design/Section
Printed in Hong Kong by South Sea International Press

Library of Congress Cataloging-in-Publication Data

Fusek Peters, Andrew
      Strange and spooky stories / written and selected by Andrew Fusek
Peters : with illustrations by Zdenka Kabátová-Táborská.
            p.   cm.
      Contents: Otesahnek the wooden doll (Czech Republic) –– The woman
who tricked death (Central Europe) –– A very scary ghost story
(Ireland) –– The tall one, the broad one, and the sharp-eyed one
(Czech Republic) –– The hungry farmer (North America) –– The talking
skull (Africa) –– The boy who could not touch the ground (Czech
Republic) –– Simon and the fish (Ireland) –– Three standing stones
(England)
      Summary: Traditional scary stories from various countries.
      ISBN 0-7613-0321-9 (lib. bdg.)
      1. Horror tales.   [1. Folklore.   2. Horror stories.]
I. Kabátová-Táborská, Zdenka, ill.   II. Title.
PZ8.1.P525St   1997
398.2 –– dc21   97—3270
                                                                  CIP
                                                                  AC

Strange and Spooky Stories

retold by

Andrew Fusek Peters

with illustrations by

Zdenka Kabátová-Táborská

THE MILLBROOK PRESS

BROOKFIELD, CONNECTICUT

Contents

Foreword

In my work over the years as a storyteller and writer for children of all ages, there are certain stories that have become favorites with my young listeners. These tales tend to be the stranger, sillier, spookier, and more surreal of the stories I know, often with a weird twist at the end. They are filled with unlikely heroes and heroines, odd images, and some truly frightening moments.

The nine stories in this book are the best I know of these tried and tested tales. They have been gathered from all over the world – from Central Europe, North America, Africa, Great Britain, and also the Far Coast of Imagination. All of them are traditional tales that have been told and retold by generations of storytellers, with each storyteller inventing a new way to bring them to life.

In all of the tales, fantastic things happen – statues move, a skull talks, babies eat sheep, a man falls in love with a fish, and Death himself is tricked! As for what happens in *A Very Scary Ghost Story* – well, you will have to find out for yourself!

Happy reading, but make sure you look under your bed before the lights go out!

Andrew Fusek Peters

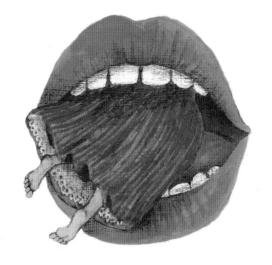

Otesahnek the Wooden Doll

A man and a woman wanted to have a baby, but they could not. The man was a woodworker by trade, and his job was to carve old branches that he found into the shapes of squirrels, foxes, and owls. One day as he was walking in the forest, he found a tree stump that looked just like a baby! He took it home and began to carve it with his knife. He carved for one night, for two nights, for three nights...until, on the fourth morning, as the sun opened her bright eyes, the wooden baby shivered and began to scream.

And the first words he said were:

"I am Otesahnek the wooden doll, and I'm hungry!"

Quickly, the mother went to the big stove and prepared a great pot of porridge. Otesahnek ate one bowl, then two bowls, then three bowls. He turned to his mother and screamed:

"I am Otesahnek the wooden doll, and I'm hungry!"

Quickly, the mother went back to the stove and began to prepare some chicken soup. Otesahnek ate one bowl, then two bowls, then three bowls. He turned to his mother and screamed:

"I am Otesahnek the wooden doll, and I'm hungry! I ate the porridge, I ate the soup, and now I'm going to eat you!"

With that he opened his mouth so wide that the mother fell inside. Now, the father had been outside chopping wood for the fire. He came back in and saw that Otesahnek had grown and grown until he was now the size of the stove. The wooden doll turned to his father and screamed:

"I am Otesahnek the wooden doll, and I'm hungry! I ate the porridge, I ate the soup, I ate my mother, and now I'm going to eat you!"

With that, he opened his mouth so wide that the father fell inside. Otesahnek was now as big as a door and found it very hard squeezing out of the house. And he was still hungry! He had been walking in the woods for only a few minutes, when he came upon a little girl pushing a wheelbarrow full of cabbages.

"Who are you?" she cried.

"I am Otesahnek the wooden doll, and I'm hungry! I ate the porridge, I ate the soup, I ate my mother, I ate my father, and now I'm going to eat you!"

With that, he opened his mouth so wide that the little girl fell inside, followed by the wheelbarrow and cabbages one by one by one. Now Otesahnek was the size of a house! And he was still hungry! He came to the edge of the woods. Beyond the trees stood a farmer in the middle of his field of golden corn.

"Who are you?" he cried.

"I am Otesahnek the wooden doll, and I'm hungry! I ate the porridge, I ate the soup, I ate my mother, I ate my father, I ate the little girl, I ate the wheelbarrow, I ate the cabbages one by one by one, and now I'm going to eat you!"

With that, he opened his mouth so wide that the farmer fell inside, followed by the golden ears of corn one by one by one. Now Otesahnek was the size of a cloud! And he was still hungry! He came to the edge of the empty field. Beyond, there stood a shepherd in a meadow with his sheep.

"Who are you?" he cried.

"I am Otesahnek the wooden doll, and I'm hungry! I ate the porridge, I ate the soup, I ate my mother, I ate my father, I ate the little girl, I ate the wheelbarrow, I ate the cabbages, I ate the farmer and his golden ears of corn one by one by one, and now I'm going to eat you!"

With that, he opened his mouth so wide that the shepherd fell inside, followed by the sheep who hopped in one by one by one. Now Otesahnek was the size of the sky! And he was still hungry. He walked for one day, for two days, for three days until he came to a small wood. By the wood was a small cottage. By the small cottage was a small garden. In the small garden was a small woman, so old and wrinkled she looked like a raisin. She looked up from hoeing her vegetables with her sharp and trusty hoe.

"Who are you?" she demanded.

"I am Otesahnek the wooden doll, and I'm hungry! I ate the porridge, I ate the soup, I ate my mother, I ate my father, I ate the little girl, I ate the wheelbarrow, I ate the cabbages, I ate the farmer, I ate the golden ears of corn, I ate the shepherd and his sheep one by one by one, and now I'm going to eat you!"

"No, you are not!" she shouted, and she cut his tummy open with her sharp and trusty hoe. And out came the porridge, and out came the soup, and out walked the mother, and out ran the father, and out skipped the little girl with her wheelbarrow full of cabbages, and out strode the farmer with his field of golden corn all cut and baled, and out danced the shepherd who whistled for his sheep to come one by one by one...

Until all that was left of Otesahnek was a little tree root. So! Be careful about what you wish for, or you could find yourself in Big Trouble!

The Woman Who Tricked Death

Now there was once a young woman who had no work, which was a bit of a problem since she wanted to be rich. Well, it just happened, as these things do, that one day there was a knock on the door. Who was it then, do you think? None other than old Death himself. How could you tell? He was skinny, really skinny, so skinny he had no skin. Just a lot of bone beneath his black suit. His face looked a bit pale, and he didn't have any eyes. Definitely Death. No doubt about it.

He said to the woman: "You want to be rich? No problem, my dear lady! Just make some business cards calling yourself a doctor. And when you go to visit the poor patients, don't worry – I'll be there. Here's the trick of it. If I am standing at the head of the bed, that patient will get

better by you simply laying your soft hand on his or her head. But if I am standing at the foot of the bed – forget it. That patient is mine until the end of time!"

Death smiled while he was talking. He had a lot of teeth. The woman agreed to the plan, though she wondered why Death was trying to help her. But it was something to keep her busy. She made some cards and gave them out, waiting for the phone to ring. And ring it did, one dark night. She was called out to the poorest of poor areas of the city and came to a one-room shack. A ragged, worried mother pushed her into the house. The rotten door gave way to a damp and cold inside. In the single bed lay a young skinny man, not looking well at all, eyes closed and waiting to die.

Guess who was standing at the head of the bed? Definitely Death! No doubt about it! Quick as a thought, she put her hand on the boy's head. He opened his eyes, and the mother jumped for joy. Death smiled and the woman went home.

Next day, the phone rang. It was a rich man's house, this time – in the nice part of town. Plenty of rooms, carpets so thick you could sleep on them. The woman was led up the stairs and into a well-decorated room, to see the man's wife not looking well at all. Her eyes were closed and she was waiting to die.

Can you guess who was standing at the head of the bed? Definitely Death. No doubt about it! Quick as an eel, she put her hand on the wife's head. She opened her eyes, and the rich man jumped right up in the air for joy. Then he gave her a bag of silver. Death smiled and the woman went home.

Word about the miracle doctor spread like Chinese whispers. And every time she went to a house, guess who was standing at the head of the bed? Definitely Death! No doubt about it! Soon she was rich as rich can be and richer still. The only thing missing in her life was a little bit of love.

She was dreaming about the perfect man in her life when the phone rang. It was the king! Not a doubt in the world that it was the king himself!

"My son is ill!" he said in a very royal voice. "And the wise women and wise men have tried their utmost. Potions, spells, pills, and exercises. Nothing has worked, and soon my son shall be nothing also. If you can cure him, his hand shall be yours in marriage, as shall half of my kingdom. But if you cannot," the King thundered, "then you shall return home without that which sits on top of your shoulders – your head!"

The woman had no worry in the world. Why, Death always stood at the head of the bed. This would be a very simple task indeed. So she dressed up in her finest clothes, dabbed a bit of perfume behind each ear

18

and made her way to the castle. The grand gates of gold opened before her. She was led through stone corridors wider and longer than rivers, up great stairs of marble until she came to the prince's bedroom, which was large enough to contain a house.

In the center stood an enormous four-poster bed, fashioned from four oak trees. Each corner had a little wheel on it, to help move the bed for cleaning. The prince was hidden from view behind curtains of rich green velvet. Without saying a word, the king strode across the room to his son's bed and drew back the curtains.

And guess who was standing at the foot of the bed? Definitely Death! No doubt about it! And he was smiling a toothy smile. What could the poor woman do? She was in despair! She would lose her head! She thought and she thought and she thought, until she had a flash of inspiration. A light bulb appeared on top of her head. She threw it away and, quick as a shooting star, she swiveled the bed right around, until Death was standing at the head of the bed. Before he could say anything, she put her hand on the young man's forehead. The prince opened his eyes. It was love at first sight.

These things happen very fast. They got married that night, with a big feast of eating, drinking, and dancing. The new princess was as happy as the sun. The morning came and they rode off out of the castle to take their lands as man and wife.

Now guess who came swooping out of the sky? Definitely Death! No doubt about it! He grabbed the princess before she could cry, "Wait a

second!" and whipped her up into the sky, past the clouds, by the sun, through the stars, down the Milky Way, into a darkness so dark there was nothing to be seen, until at last they came to a door.

"After you, my lady!" Death bowed as she opened the door. Behind was a vast room, full of flickering oil lamps. "These are all the lives of all the people in all the universe! When the oil runs out, they die, and it's my job to tend the lamps." He reached up onto one shelf and pulled out various lamps, filled with various amounts of oil. Each of them was marked with the different stages of life, from IMMORTAL at the top, down to VERY OLD AND NOT MUCH TIME LEFT. Then he held up one lamp in which the oil just reached up to the words FIVE MINUTES LEFT TO LIVE. "This, my dear lady, is your lamp! I'm ever so sorry!" Death smiled.

What could she do? She was in despair! She would lose her life! She thought and she thought and she thought, until she had a flash of inspiration. A light bulb appeared on top of her head. She threw it away and, quick as a bolt of lightning, she turned to Death.

"Dear Death, seeing as I am to die in only five minutes, maybe I could tell you a story to pass the time?" She smiled sweetly, and Death agreed it would be a pleasurable thing to listen to a short tale. He settled his bony frame into an old armchair stuffed with human hair, and she began to tell him a tale about how there was this young woman who had no work and wanted to be rich. One day there was a knock on the door and...

But her story was really very boring. So boring and dull, in fact, that Death began to yawn politely and then found himself falling into a deep, deep snooze. By the end of the tale, Death was snoring away, the breath whistling through his pearly white teeth.

This is just what the young woman wanted. She ran to the oil jar, filled up her lamp and the lamp of the prince to the level marked IMMORTAL. Death slept on, as she crept out of the room through the darkness so dark there was nothing to be seen, down the Milky Way, through the stars, by the sun, past the clouds, into the sky, and back onto the horse she had left only a second before. The prince had not even noticed that she had gone.

And guess what? They rode off into the new day, and lived happily ever after. Definitely in love! No doubt about it!

A Very Scary Ghost Story

Far away, on the west coast of Connemara in the country of Ireland, when the sun falls from the sky the mist comes rolling in from the sea like a carpet. On such a night, not so long ago, an old man was getting ready for bed. He lived all alone in a big house, for his wife had died some years before, and his nearest neighbor was five miles away. As he was closing the wooden shutters on the windows, he heard a strange sound coming from beyond the garden, out in the thick mist:

I am the Ghost of Bleeding Finger, coming, coming, coming!

He was ever so scared – but maybe it was just a trick of the wind? Anyway, he quickly bolted the front door, ran upstairs, and dived under his bed. Then he heard the garden gate screeching open: *eeeeeeeeeehhhhh!*

The hinges were rusty and needed oiling. There were footsteps up the garden path:

I am the Ghost of Bleeding Finger, coming, coming, coming!

He shivered under his bed, as he heard the door that he had just bolted screeching slowly open: *eeeeeeeeeehhhhh!* The hinges were rusty and needed oiling. There were footsteps across the corridor downstairs:

I am the Ghost of Bleeding Finger, coming, coming, coming!

He shivered under the bed, but what could he do? There were footsteps coming up the stairs toward the bedroom door:

I am the Ghost of Bleeding Finger, coming, coming, coming!

The footsteps stopped outside the door – he was scared enough to drop dead of fright. The door screeched slowly, ever so slowly, open: *eeeeeeeeeehhhhh!* The hinges were rusty and needed oiling. The footsteps came across the floor toward the bed:

I am the Ghost of Bleeding Finger, coming, coming, coming!

The voice was right above him now. He shook with fear, but where could he run to? The voice boomed louder now, as the bed was pushed away and a face appeared above him and screamed in agony:

I am the Ghost of Bleeding Finger! Have you got a bandage? My finger is really hurting!

The Tall One, the Broad One, and the Sharp-Eyed One

The prince wanted to fall in love. He had no idea how to do this, so he went to ask his father the king. The king gave him a key and told him to go up into the far tower of the castle, where the prince had never been before. The prince ran through the long drafty corridors until he came to the spiral stone stairs that squeezed up into the tower. Around and up he went, becoming dizzier and dizzier. At last he saw a door painted bright blue. The key fit perfectly and the door swung open.

The room was dimly lit, as if it were twilight, and had twelve corners. In each of the twelve corners but the last stood statues of princesses from all over the world. In the last corner hung a curtain of green velvet. The prince

28

was not interested in these statues, and out of curiosity pulled on the curtain. It fell away to reveal the most beautiful princess, carved so delicately the stone almost breathed. The prince was in love! He ran out the door, down the stairs, and through the corridors until he came to his father.

When the king heard who his son had fallen in love with, he sighed: "Why did you have to chose her, my boy? There are plenty of other princesses! This lady you are in love with has been captured by the Iron Sorcerer. And now you will have to rescue her!"

Of course, the prince had no idea how to do this, but he went valiantly out of the castle ready to do great deeds. Soon he was lost. Worse, he was in the middle of the wood. Just then, he spied a very tall woman leaning against an even taller tree.

"Good day to you, sir! Are you lost?" she said in a high-pitched voice. "I will help you on your way if you wish, for I am the Tall One!" And with that she stretched up and up until her head was taller than the tallest leaf and she could see out of the forest.

"You can help me on my quest!" the prince shouted up at her.

"And I have a friend who will be of great use!" she replied, pointing to the middle of the field. There the prince saw a very large, round, short man.

"I am the Broad One!" the man shouted, "and beware as I take a breath!"

Then he took a huge breath, which made him so big that he squashed the whole field.

"You can help me on my quest!" the prince shouted at the Broad One.

"And I have a friend who will be of great use," replied the man, pointing

to the far corner of the field. There stood a man with a blindfold over his eyes.

"I am the Sharp-Eyed One!" said the man in a low voice, taking off his blindfold. "Too much sight pains me! But dear prince, I can easily see the greasy handkerchief, the gold ring as a present to the one you love, the wind-up horse as a toy, a comb, and a mirror, all in your left pocket!" The prince was very embarrassed. He must wash his handkerchief soon. He was also impressed.

"You can help me on my quest!" he said gladly and, without further ado, they set off over the land.

They crossed many hills and valleys, swam rivers, climbed some mountains and generally took a long time about getting to their destination. A month had passed, and they were crossing a small bridge leading to a very strange castle. The walls were rusting and everything was a dark metal color. The portcullis was open as they came into the courtyard.

It was as if someone had frozen all time and turned it to iron in the middle of a moment. For there was a bustle about the courtyard: pages preparing, servants running, piemen serving pies, jugglers juggling, even poets declaiming. But the pages did not move, the servants ran in place, the pies of the piemen were rusting not steaming, the clubs of the jugglers hung suspended in the air, and the poet could not get a word out.

The prince and his friends walked slowly past them toward the door of the great hall. The door slid open silently and they crept in. In the hall stood the Iron Sorcerer. He was as stout as a barrel and had three iron bands around his chest to keep him from falling apart. By his side and not looking very happy was the princess. She looked up and met the eyes of the prince. He was quite handsome, she thought.

"I have come for the hand of the princess!" demanded the prince.

"But her hand is her own!" boomed the Iron Sorcerer. "Yet will I give you a chance. If you can keep her under your eyes for three days and three nights, then I will give her to you, if she will have you, for in my house

she is a most unwilling prisoner!" As he finished speaking, the Sorcerer turned about and walked through the door, slamming it behind him.

It was all simple. They were not to let her out of their sight through day or night. So the Tall One stretched up and wrapped herself around the hall three times, the Broad One took a huge breath and filled every nook and cranny, and the Sharp-Eyed One kept a look-out.

The day fell away and the night woke up. And as night stretched herself across the sky, one by one the prince and his friends just went to sleep. Then the moon shone onto the prince's face. He opened his eyes and looked around. The princess had gone! Quickly he woke the others, but no one could find her except the Sharp-Eyed One, who saw her turned into an acorn at the tip of an Oak tree just outside the castle gates.

The Tall One reached up, stretching her arm out of an arrow slit at the top of the hall, plucked the acorn off the tree, and pulled it back into the hall. She opened her hand and it fell to the ground. As it landed, the acorn changed back into the princess. Dawn broke, like an egg, and the Iron Sorcerer strode in, feeling very happy with himself. When he saw the princess, it was such a shock that one of his iron bands burst with a clang.

"Two more nights!" he boomed angrily, turned about and walked through the door, slamming it behind him.

They were not to let her out of their sight through day or night. So, the Tall One stretched up and wrapped herself around the hall three times, the Broad One took a huge breath and filled every nook and cranny, and the Sharp-Eyed One kept a look-out.

The day flew faster than the wind, and soon night ran in, even faster than day. She covered the sky in the blink of an eye. As the eyes of the day closed in darkness, one by one, the prince and his friends fell fast asleep. Then the moon smiled down onto the prince's face. He woke up and looked around. The princess had gone! He shook the others awake but no one could find her, except for the Sharp-Eyed One. She had been turned into a drop of dew hanging on a blade of grass just outside the castle gates.

The Tall One stretched her arm up and out of the arrow slit and down to the blade of grass. She shook it like a bell and the drop of dew fell into her hand. She unstretched back into the hall and opened her hand like a petal. The drop of dew fell and with a splash turned back into the princess.

Dawn opened her mouth and light sang across the sky. The Iron Sorcerer strode in, feeling very happy with himself. When he saw the princess, it was such a shock that the second of his iron bands burst with a clang.

"One more night!" he boomed angrily, turned about and walked through the door, slamming it behind him.

They were not to let her out of their sight through day or night. So, the Tall One stretched up and wrapped herself around the hall three times, the Broad One took a huge breath and filled every nook and cranny, and the Sharp-Eyed One kept a look-out.

Well, the day just disappeared, for night had come at last to steal it. And, as the sun went into her bag, the sky turned dark. One by one the prince and his friends fell fast asleep. Then the moon crept across the prince's face, as quiet as silver. The prince woke up and looked around. The princess had gone! He shook all his friends awake but no one could find her.

Even the Sharp-Eyed One was at a loss. Then he looked out across the lands to the sea beyond and saw her hidden away as a golden ring in a shipwreck at the bottom of an ocean. The Tall One stretched her arm up and out of the arrow slit and over the clouds and down to the ocean's edge. But the water was just too deep and she just could not stretch that far.

However, the Broad One had an idea. The Tall One picked up the prince, the Sharp-Eyed One, and the Broad One, squeezed them through the narrow window, and dropped them on the beach. The Broad One opened his mouth, leaned over, drank half the ocean, and closed his mouth as tight as tight can be. The Tall One then stretched her arm again, and this time reached down easily into the shallow water to pick the ring from the wreck. As she pulled it out of the water and dropped it onto the beach, the shining golden ring transformed into the shining golden princess, and the prince was very much in love.

They did not have much time, as the day was threatening to burst across the night sky. The Tall One was exhausted with all the lifting and stretching, so they had to run as fast as they could back toward the castle. On their way they came across a very small branch, so small it was a twig and the twig was so small it was a twiglet.

Unfortunately, the Broad One tripped over it and opened his mouth to cry out. As he did, half the ocean fell out and they all nearly drowned. It took them a long time to swim to safety, and when they finally arrived back at the castle, the sun was sneaking over the edge of the mountains. In the hall, the Iron Sorcerer was waiting for them and smiling happily to himself. The princess was running behind the Broad One, so the Sorcerer could not see her.

"You have not found her!" he boomed, "and so she is mine!"

"I most certainly am not!" declared the princess, stepping out from behind the Broad One.

"What?!" said the Sorcerer, in complete shock, as he burst the last of his iron bands. "What!?" he cried, as he crumpled into a pile of iron filings. The Tall One, the Broad One, and the Sharp-Eyed One let out a cheer and the castle came back to life.

The piemen's pies were steaming and hot, the pages carried on preparing, the jugglers' clubs danced through the air, and the poet declaimed the whole story most brilliantly.

And the prince and princess? Well... if you must know, they fell in complete and utter love, kissed a lot, got married, and lived happily ever after.

The Hungry Farmer

The farmer and his wife were growing old. The farm was not going well, and bit by bit they had to sell off their land until they had only one field left. And a poor field it was. They were always hungry, but what could they do?

The farmer thought hard and long. He so much wanted to cook a lovely meal for his wife. But apart from a few potatoes and some greens, the larder was bare. There was nothing for it. He would have to go and shoot some dinner for the pot. Into the livingroom he came. It was cold, for there was no fire in the grate. He reached above the mantelpiece. On the wall was a gun, the oldest gun you have ever seen. It had been his father's and his father's before him.

He went out the door and walked toward the woods. The sun was beginning to tire, and her sleepy face was lying on the far hills. The farmer put some powder on the tinder plate. He did not have to wait long. There! Filling the sky flew a flock of geese with their necks stretched out into the night. And with the geese came a sound unlike any he had heard before. It was as if the trees themselves had begun singing to him. He looked around him to find where the sound came from. And then he knew it. It was the geese. He wanted to stay and listen forever.

But the farmer's hunger was calling to him. With great difficulty, he raised the gun to his shoulders and pointed at the flying flock. There was a huge crash, like drums and cymbals all together, and one of the birds began to fall slowly toward the ground. Still there was the haunting music. He ran to the dead bird and picked it up. The rest of the geese flew off in alarm, but still the music sounded.

He went home and plucked the bird to make it ready for the oven. With the music in his ears, it was the hardest thing to do, and he felt so close to tears. The oven was hot and the cooking began. Outside the window, stars filled the sky. Now, at last, the music began to fade, and the smell of the goose made the farmer lick his lips. He invited his wife into the kitchen and sat her down.

The farmer was about to carve when he found he could not move. Suddenly, there was a sound. The sound grew louder and the farmer's wife began to smile. It was just like a song she remembered from when she was a little girl. Tears began to run down her face. The music grew louder. Still, the farmer could not move.

The window blew open with a crash like drums and cymbals all together, and the room was filled with geese flying around above the table in a great, slow-moving circle.

One of them bent her long, fine neck and plucked a feather from her back. Then she dived and placed the feather on the back of the dead goose on the table. One by one, the other geese curved their necks and pulled single feathers from their backs to cover the dead bird.

The music stopped. There was a moment of silence. Then, the dead bird began to move, gently at first, trying its new wings, flapping them slightly, then with more confidence. The air was filled with musical notes, and the farmer and his wife could only look on in wonder as the newly reborn bird rose out of the pan to join its friends. The circle broke, and the flock of geese flew out of the window into the night, leaving only an echo of the music.

The spell had been broken. The farmer and his wife were still hungry. But what could they eat? As if in answer to the question, his wife pointed at the pan. There among the potatoes and greens, lay two large, pearl-white goose eggs. They smiled in joy and sat down to eat a feast that night as the geese flew off to other times and other lands.

The Talking Skull

A hunter went into the bush to hunt. But all he found in the dusty old desert was the skull of a dead man.

"What brought you here?" asked the hunter.

The skull answered him: "Talking brought me here!"

The hunter was very excited and ran back to the king. He told the king: "I found the skull of a dead man in the desert! It was a talking skull! And it asked me how your mother and father are!"

"Never since my mother gave me life have I heard of a skull that can speak!" The king then summoned the wise men of his kingdom – the Saba, the Alkali, the Degi. He asked them all if they had ever heard of a talking skull. None of the wise men had ever heard of such a thing. So a

guard was sent out with the hunter, back into the desert, to see if the hunter was telling the truth. The guard was ordered to kill the hunter if he was found to be lying to the king.

The guard and hunter set off across the dunes until at last they came to the skull. The hunter spoke out: "Skull! Speak to me as you did earlier this day!"

The skull said nothing.

The hunter spoke out again: "Skull! What brought you here?"

The skull stayed silent all day. As the sun set, the guard, who only saw a silent skull, turned to the hunter and killed him.

When the guard was gone, the skull opened its jaws and asked the dead hunter: "What brought you here?"

The dead hunter answered: "Talking brought me here!"

The Boy Who Could Not Touch the Ground

In the village of Valesky Klobouky, in Moravia, there lived not so long ago, a rich landowner and his fine wife. Their house was more than large enough, and the gardens spread for acres. They had everything their hearts could desire, except a child. How they prayed! How they hoped! But no child came to ease their loneliness.

Until, in the dark of one October night, the husband had a dream. He dreamed that his wife had given birth to a beautiful baby boy! The dream also contained a warning:

The boy must not touch the ground for twelve whole years.

Behold, in time the wife did indeed give birth to a splendid baby boy.

52

Taking heed of his dream, her husband hired twelve good nursemaids to carry and cradle the boy, that his feet might never feel the earth until he was twelve years old.

They did the job well and no disasters befell the child. He was now one day short of twelve years and there was a great hustling and bustling in the big house in preparation for his birthday feast. The boy's legs had been stretched and pulled, so that they would be ready for the job of carrying him after all these years.

It was late afternoon and the sun shone in long beams through the boy's bedroom windows. The nursemaid in charge at the time was quite bored and her arms ached. Then she heard a commotion down in the courtyard below. The stable lad had been caught picking the pockets of the coachman. There was a great to-do as the fat coachman roared around the yard with his whip, desperate to catch and punish the eel-like stable lad. The nursemaid was so curious that she had to get a better look. Without thinking, she put the landowner's son on the floor and

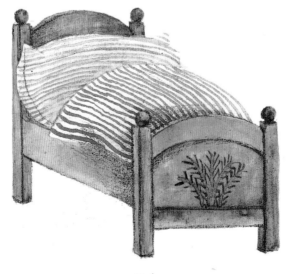

54

flew over to the window to open it. Finally, the stable lad was caught and his cries sang out across the yard! The nursemaid smiled and turned around to pick the boy up again.

But he had gone! She screamed and peered under the bed. She cried out and looked in the cupboard. She ran down the corridors in tears to tell the mother and father. And the landowner remembered his dream. They searched high and they searched low, but the boy had gone. The nursemaids were all dismissed and the father brooded on his ruin.

Night came and found the father pacing up and down the corridors. The clock began to strike the twelfth hour, and at the last stroke the landowner happened to be passing his son's bedroom. In the silence, a wail broke out unlike any sound he had ever heard. The landowner might have been the richest of men, but he was not the bravest, and he ran as fast as his little legs would carry him, into the arms of his wife.

The next morning, at his wife's suggestion, the father issued a proclamation in the town, which stated:

Whosoever can stay the whole night in my son's bedroom will be rewarded with the sum of three hundred golden kroner.

The krone was the type of coin used in that part of Moravia, and three hundred kroner was a small fortune.

As luck would have it, there lived at the end of the town a miller's widow and her three daughters. They often had to go without food and their lives were difficult. The eldest daughter had heard the

proclamation and asked her mother if she could go to the landowner's house. It was only for a night, after all, she argued. Nothing terrible could happen...

The mother saw nothing amiss in this, and the eldest daughter found her way up to the big house, where she knocked nervously on the front door. The landowner answered, and he was only too glad to let the girl stay.

"I am hungry," she said, "and I have not eaten all day. Please give me some food!" And so a servant was sent to the pantry. He returned with: *meat, bread, flour, water, salt, a pot to cook in, firewood, and a beeswax candle.*

Up went the girl to the boy's room. And what with the laying of the fire and the table, the making of the bed and the cooking of the food, the clock soon began to strike twelve. As silence fell again, a wailing broke out, unlike any sound she had ever heard. Though terrified, she stood her ground. The sound faded away and there stood a young boy with a pale face.

"For whom have you made this bed?" he asked.

"For myself, of course!" she replied. He frowned and asked a second question.

"For whom have you laid the table?"

"For myself, of course!" she replied. Tears began to fall from his eyes as he asked finally:

"And for whom did you cook this meal?"

"For myself, of course!" she replied. And the boy began to fade back into nothing, the tears still streaming down his face. The eldest daughter thought no more about this as she was hungry. She ate the food, went to bed, and in the morning claimed her three hundred kroner.

The next day, the second daughter decided to try her luck. She asked her mother, who thought that six hundred kroner would be even better than three hundred.

So off she went up the hill and knocked nervously on the front door of the landowner's house. The boy's mother came anxiously to the door, and was glad when the girl asked if she could stay.

"And please, could I also have some food, as I am hungry and have not eaten all day?" The boy's mother nodded her head and sent the servant to the pantry to bring out: *meat, bread, flour, salt, a pot to cook in, firewood, and a beeswax candle.*

Up went the girl to the boy's room, and what with the laying of the fire and the table, the making of the bed and the cooking of the food, the clock was soon striking twelve. At the twelfth stroke, a silence fell, broken only by a wailing unlike any sound she had ever heard. The girl was terrified and could not move. The wailing faded and there stood a young boy.

"For whom have you made this bed?" he asked.

"For myself, of course!" she replied. The boy grew sad.

"For whom have you laid the table?"

"For myself, of course!" she replied. The boy grew sadder.

"And for whom have you made this meal?"

"Why, for myself, of course!" she said, becoming quite annoyed. The boy burst into tears and, disappeared before her eyes. She thought no more about it as the food smelled delicious. The daughter ate, went to bed, and in the morning rightly claimed her three hundred Kroner.

The next day came, and the youngest daughter of the widow thought to try her fortune. She was curious and concerned about this boy who had vanished. Her mother was quite happy for her to go, too. For nine hundred golden kroner was a queenly sum indeed!

Off went the girl, climbing up the hill to knock without fear on the door of the house. The landowner answered the door, to see a girl the same age as his son. His heart felt heavy, but he welcomed her in.

"Please, if you could provide me with some food, I would be most grateful," she said gently. The servant was sent to the pantry and brought out: *meat, bread, flour, salt, a pot to cook in, firewood, and a beeswax candle.*

The girl was led to the bedroom and set to work. And what with the laying of the fire and the table, the making of the bed and the cooking of the food, all too soon the clock was striking twelve. As silence fell, a wailing broke out, unlike any sound she had ever heard. It seemed so sad, and when it finished, a boy stood in the middle of the room. He looked into her eyes:

"For whom have you made this bed?" he asked with hope in his voice.

"For myself, but if you are tired, you can rest on the bed and I shall sleep on the couch!" she replied. He smiled and his eyes grew bright.

"For whom have you laid this table?" he asked.

"For myself, but you can sit with me!" she replied. The boy wanted to shout for joy!

"And for whom have you made this meal?"

"For myself, but you can share it with me!" she replied. And the boy did not disappear, nor float off the ground.

"Thank God that someone still cares for me in this house! I must go and thank those who have been looking after me. Please wait for me and we shall eat together!"

As he finished speaking, a hole appeared in the floor, filled with light. The boy turned his back and began to sink down. The youngest daughter crept up behind the boy and grabbed hold of his coattails to follow him down.

They came to a different land that could not be, but was. The girl crept behind the boy, following closely in his footsteps as he walked toward a forest made of gold. Birds came out of the trees to sit on his arms and hands. He thanked each one in turn, and the trees parted to reveal a path. The girl picked up a small gold twig to show that she had been there and followed until they came to a lake made of silver. Many fish came to say goodbye to the boy, and he thanked each one in turn. While the boy was busy talking to the fishes in the lake, the youngest daughter quietly took out a perfume bottle she always carried and filled it with silver water, to show that she had been there. When he had said his last goodbye, the boy turned back and began to float upward through the golden hole. The youngest daughter grabbed hold of his coattails again, and they were in the bedroom once more. The floor closed like a door and they sat down to eat by the warm fire.

Morning came and the sun knew it would be a good day. As the landowner and his wife had not heard a sound from the girl, they became concerned and burst into the room to see a sight that filled their hearts. Their son had returned! The boy awoke and embraced his parents. "Where have you been?" they cried, but he would not answer. Instead, he turned and spoke quietly to the miller's daughter:

"I know that you followed me and it is a good thing, as you shall see. Take the golden twig and throw it out of the window!" She did as he bade, and the wind whirled it around and around until it landed on a far hill, where up sprang a golden castle.

"Now take the water and let the wind carry it!" And so she did, and the wind whirled the perfume bottle until it splashed its contents onto the far hill, and there sprang up a silver moat around the castle.

As it was to be, so did the boy and girl fall in love. And in time they were married, and in time they lived the longest and fullest of lives.

Simon and the Fish

Simon did not like fish. No, he hated fish. Which was a bad thing, you see, as the only job he could get was as a *fisherman*.

Now, it so happened that one day he was out in the boat with his boss, who was a mean old man. Simon's task was to pull in the nets. As he was pulling away on the nets, into the boat fell a fish unlike any you've ever seen in your life. This fish had scales all the colors of a rainbow after a storm, and they were shining as brightly as the happy sun.

Simon couldn't bring himself to kill such a beautiful fish, so with a quick flick of his hand he slipped it back into the water. As it swam away, the fish turned and gave him a big wink with one of its eyes. The mean old man of a boss saw all this, and Simon lost his job on the spot.

What would he do now, and however was he to feed his fifteen brothers and fifteen sisters?

Later that day Simon was out walking along the cliff top, when the wind did a sudden whirl and a strange figure appeared. Tall and skinny, very skinny. In fact it had no skin at all, just a lot of bones. It was Death! Simon shivered in his boots as Death spoke in a soft, deathly kind of voice:

"Now, boy, no need to be scared. I've come to help, and here is what I'll do. I will give you a cow with an endless supply of milk. All you have to do is answer three of my questions at the end of seven years, and you can keep the cow and live forever. If you can't," Death smiled, flashing his white teeth, "then you shall have to come with me!"

It sounded like a good deal. Anyhow, Simon was tired and hungry and

only wanted to get home. He grabbed Death's hand and shook it in agreement. The hand was as cold as winter and, as he shook it, the wind did a sudden whirl and Death disappeared. In his place was a big, fat cow with huge udders. Simon walked the cow home to show to his fifteen brothers and fifteen sisters.

They found a milking stool and began to milk the cow. There was so much milk that another bucket had to be fetched, and still the cow did not run out of milk. They had so much milk that they decided to make some of it into cheese to sell. Soon, they had so much money from all the cheese that they built a restaurant on the cliff top overlooking the sea far below. There was only one type of food they did not serve in the restaurant. And what was that? You've guessed it – fish!

Time passed by in rather a rush, for soon seven years had fallen away and Simon had forgotten all about Death and his questions. He was too busy running his restaurant with his fifteen brothers and fifteen sisters.

It was a Monday night. Monday night is always quiet in restaurants. The only customer was a woman wearing a dress all the colors of the rainbow. The wind did a sudden whirl outside and the door crashed open. And there stood a tall, skinny figure. Very skinny. In fact so skinny it had no skin at all, just bones. It was Death! No doubt about it! Death opened his toothy mouth to speak:

"Are you ready for your questions, Simon?"

As he spoke, the woman in the many-colored dress stood up and said:

"Yes he is! That's your first question! What's your second?"

Death was annoyed and pointed at the woman with his bony fingers:

"And is this woman doing all the talking for you?" he shouted.

"Yes, I am!" said the woman. "That's your second question! What's your third?"

Death was getting angry, and without thinking turned to the woman:

"And who in Death's name are you?" he screamed.

72

"I am Queen of all the fish in the sea! Seven years ago to this day Simon saved my life and now I am saving his! That's your third question and your last!" she sang and stuck her nose up at Death.

What could Death do? With a huff and a puff and a whirl of the wind, he disappeared to sulk for the rest of time.

Three Standing Stones

In times long ago, Arthur was King of Britain, and magic ruled the land. Merlin was the wisest of all, though as he grew old he became foolish. Now, he had three sons, handsome and tall, and wished them to be married. Merlin lived down in what has come to be called Cornwall, a finger of land that points out into the Atlantic Ocean. And in Cornwall there lived also three of the most beautiful women in the whole of the kingdom.

One day, in the middle of summer, Merlin summoned the women to the royal court. They came, and their beauty was such that it stole the people's breath from right under their noses. In front of a great assembly, Merlin announced that these women would make wonderful wives for his three sons. When they heard him, they burst out laughing. Who was

he to command them like this? And with one accord, they swished around in their long flowing skirts and stalked straight out, leaving a terrible silence behind them.

Merlin was furious. Like an angry wind, he stormed after them, out of the castle and down to the beach, where they had gathered. Then, in a fit of old-man temper, he cast a bitter spell, turning the women into three standing stones, right there on the beach.

There they stood through all the ages, both dark and light. Arthur was gone into a fairy tale and only legend remained. It was said that each midsummer's eve the stones walked into the water and changed back into women again, who washed all the stone from their skin. And if you happened to be out that night and happened to see them, you would be

in the greatest of danger – especially if you were a man. For, after all this time, the women inside the stones wanted revenge on Merlin and his kind. So each midsummer's eve, the villagers stayed well indoors, knowing better than to try their luck.

But the land was changing, and more people came to visit that part of Cornwall to find out about the past. One summer, a father and his son came to stay in a cottage just above the beach – tourists on vacation from far away. They were in the pub on midsummer's eve, the son sitting quietly in the corner, the father buying too many drinks. Everyone was talkative that night, and the locals began to tell the tale of Merlin and the Three Standing Stones. Well, when they had finished, the father declared that he didn't believe a word of it. A man of the world, he lived in the big

city and was something of a wizard himself – at making money. All this talk of ghosts was mere nonsense; old women's tittle-tattle; tall tales to pass the time of day and night...

"I'll go out myself and prove that these stones are just stones!" he boasted in a pompous and drunken voice.

The villagers smiled strange smiles into their glasses and decided it was time to help the foolish father to his bed. By now, the drink had got the better of him, and so they carried him back to the cottage, with a warning to the son to look after him during the night. Darkness was already falling uneasily over land and sea, and the villagers walked very quickly back to the safety of their houses, worried they were already stretching their luck.

All night the boy's head was filled with strange dreams about walking stones. He kept waking up and hearing his father tossing and turning in the next room. The boy wanted to run into his father's room, as he had a terrible fear that something bad was about to happen. But as the night wore on, he finally fell into a sleep so deep he could have been dead.

Just before the sun rose, there was a loud, crashing sound. The boy woke up. He ran to his father's room. The window was wide open and his father's bed lay empty. He ran in the twilight down to the beach, dreading the worst. Just as he came out onto the smooth sand, the sun began to break like shining glass across the sea. As he stopped and stared at the stones, he thought he could see one of them shift silently, then stop dead. He looked again. There was something dark at the bottom of the stones. The boy screamed out for help.

The villagers all came tumbling out like leaves and ran with the wind down to the beach. The three stones were standing absolutely still. And lying between them, twisted like seaweed, was the body of the father, dead as bone.

Later it was found at the official inquest that the man's body had been crushed, as if it had fallen from a great height onto the rocks on the beach. But there were no cliffs in that part of Cornwall, and the court decided it must have been the waves that had smashed his body against the standing stones. The villagers stayed silent, for they knew the truth.